Things

that

are

most

in the world

written BY Judi Barrett

Things
that
are
most
in the world

illustrated BY John Nickle

Aladdin Paperbacks

New York London Toronto Sydney Singapore

First Aladdin
Paperbacks edition
August 2001
Text copyright © 1998 by Judi
Barrett
Illustrations copyright © 1998 by John
Nickle

Aladdin Paperbacks
An imprint of Simon & Schuster
Children's Publishing Division
1230 Avenue of the Americas
New York, NY 10020

Also available in an Atheneum Books for Young Readers
hardcover edition
Designed by Anne Bobco
The text for this book was set in Gill Sans Bold and Psycho
Progressive.
The illustrations were rendered in acrylic paint.
Printed in Hong Kong
10 9 8 7 6 5 4 3 2

The Library of Congress has cataloged the hardcover edition
as follows:
Barrett, Judi.
Things that are most in the world / by Judi Barrett ;
Illustrated by John Nickle.—1st ed.
p.   cm.
Summary: The reader who wants to know what are the
quietest, silliest, smelliest, wiggliest things in the
world finds imaginative answers to these and other
questions about superlatives.
ISBN: 0-689-81333-3 (hc.)
[1. Vocabulary.] I. Nickle, John, ill. II. Title.
PZ7.B2752Th   1998
[E]—dc21
97-5155
ISBN: 0-689-84449-2 (Aladdin
pbk.)

To things that are the most, the least,
and everything in between
— J. B.

To Jana
"Who's the monkey?"
— J. N.

The

wiggliest

thing in the world

is

a snake ice-skating.

The

silliest

thing in the world

is

a chicken

in a frog costume.

The

quietest

thing in the world

is

a worm

chewing peanut butter.

The

prickliest

thing in the world

is

the inside of a pincushion.

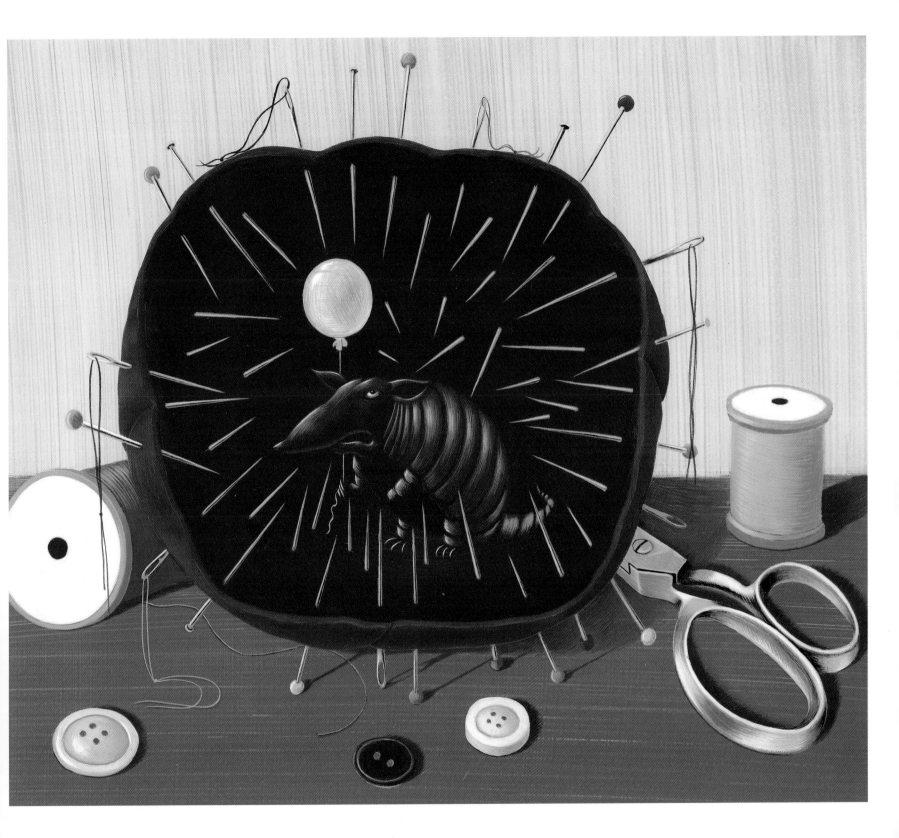

The

hottest

thing in the world

is

a fire-breathing dragon

eating a pepperoni pizza.

The

oddest

thing in the world

is

an ant windsurfing

in a bowl of pea soup.

The
teensie-weensiest
thing in the world
is
a newborn flea.

The

longest

thing in the world

is

what you'd have

if you tied every single strand

of spaghetti together

end to end.

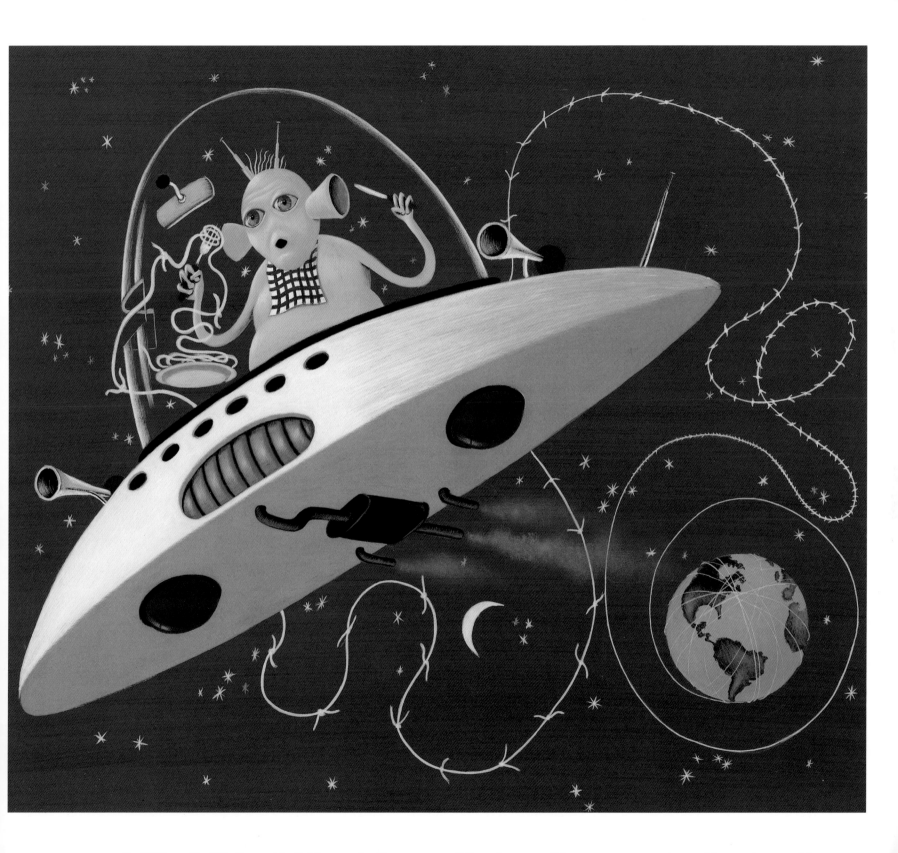

The

jumpiest

thing in the world

is

two thousand two hundred twenty-two toads

on a trampoline.

The
smelliest
thing in the world

is

a skunk convention.

The

stickiest

thing in the world

is

a 400,000-pound wad

of bubble gum.

The

heaviest

thing in the world

is

a Tyrannosaurus rex

weighing himself.

And the

highest

thing in the world

is

the very top of the sky.